First American edition 2004
by Kane/Miller Book Publishers, Inc.
La Jolla, California

Text and illustrations copyright © 2003 Chen Chih-Yuan, 2003
First published in Taiwan in 2003 under the title "Guji Guji" by Hsin Yi Publications,
Taipei, Taiwan, R.O.C. All rights reserved.
English translation published by arrangement with Hsin Yi Publications.

All rights reserved. For information contact:
Kane/Miller Book Publishers
P.O. Box 8515
La Jolla, CA 92038
www.kanemiller.com

Library of Congress Control Number: 2004100985

Printed and bound in the United States of America by Phoenix Color Corporation.

2 3 4 5 6 7 8 9 10

ISBN 1-929132-67-0

# Guji Guji

## Chih-Yuan Chen

E CHE
Chen, Zhiyuan, 1975-
Guji Guji

**Kane/Miller**
BOOK PUBLISHERS

An egg was rolling on the ground.
It rolled through the trees.
It rolled across the meadow.
It rolled all the way down the hill.

Finally, it rolled right into a duck's nest.

Mother Duck didn't notice.
(She was reading.)

Soon enough, the eggs began to crack.
The first duckling to hatch had blue spots.
Mother Duck called him Crayon.
The second duckling had brown stripes.
"Zebra," Mother Duck decided.
The third duckling was yellow, and Mother
Duck named him Moonlight.

A rather odd-looking duckling hatched
from the fourth egg. **"Guji Guji,"** he said,
and that became his name.

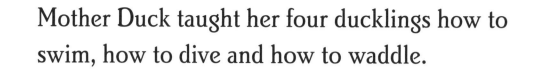

Mother Duck taught her four ducklings how to swim, how to dive and how to waddle.

Guji Guji always learned more quickly than the others.
He was bigger and stronger, too.

But no matter how quick they were, or
what they looked like, Mother Duck
loved all her ducklings the same.

Then one terrible day, three crocodiles came out of the lake. They looked a lot like Guji Guji. The crocodiles were smiling, and when they laughed with their mouths wide open, the whole world could see their big, pointed teeth.

The three crocodiles saw Guji Guji and smiled some more. "Look at that ridiculous crocodile. He's walking like a duck!"

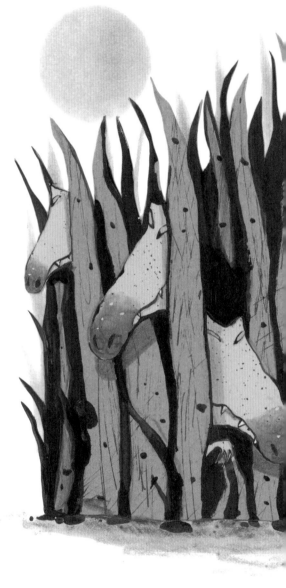

Guji Guji heard them. "I am not walking *like* a duck, I *am* a duck!" he explained.

The crocodiles laughed. "Look at yourself! No feathers, no beak, no big webbed feet! What you have is blue-gray skin, sharp claws, pointed teeth and the smell of bad crocodile. You're just like us."

The first crocodile said, "Your blue-gray body lets you hide under water without being seen so you can get close to fat, delicious ducks."

The second crocodile said, "Big, sharp claws help you hold fat, delicious ducks tightly so they don't get away."

The third crocodile said, "Pointed teeth are necessary so you can chew fat, delicious ducks. Mmmm. Yum."

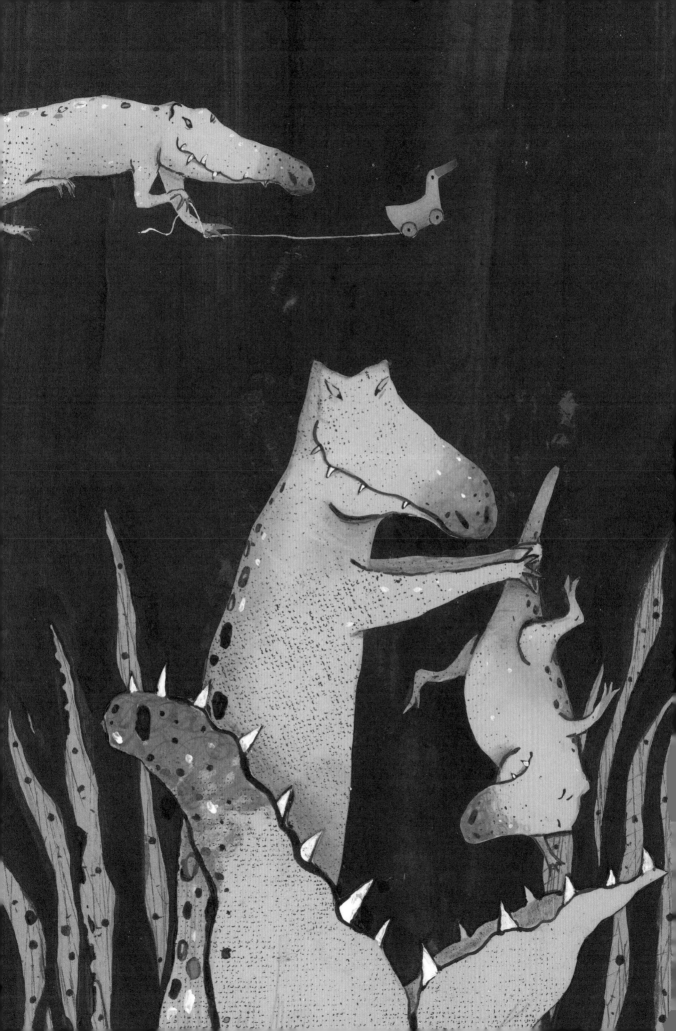

The three crocodiles grinned. "We know you live with the ducks. Take them to the bridge tomorrow and practice diving. We'll wait underneath with our mouths open wide."

"Why would I do that?" Guji Guji asked. "Why should I listen to you?"

"Because we are all crocodiles, and crocodiles help each other." The bad crocodiles grinned again and vanished into the grass.

Guji Guji felt terrible.
He sat by the lake to think.
"Is it true? Am I a bad
crocodile too?" He looked
down into the lake and
made a fierce face.
Guji Guji laughed.
He looked ridiculous.
"I am not a bad crocodile.
Of course, I'm not exactly
a duck either."

"But the three crocodiles are nasty, and they want to eat my family. I must think of a way to stop them."

Guji Guji thought and thought until finally he thought up a good idea. He went home happy and content.

That night, the three bad crocodiles sharpened their pointed teeth, all the while thinking of fat, delicious ducks. They were ready for their feast.

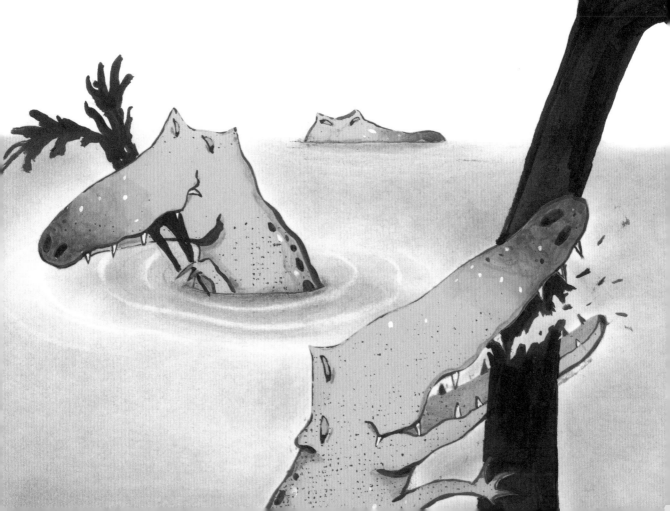

The next day, Guji Guji did as he'd been told — he took the flock of ducks to the bridge to practice diving.

The three bad crocodiles were waiting for
the ducks underneath the bridge.

It wasn't fat, delicious ducks that dropped from the bridge though; it was three big, hard rocks!

The crocodiles bit down. "Crack! Crack! Crack!" went their pointed teeth.
The three bad crocodiles ran as fast as they could.
In barely a minute, they were nowhere to be seen!

Guji Guji had saved the ducks! Guji Guji
was the duck hero of the day! That night,
all the ducks danced and celebrated.

Guji Guji continued to live with Mother Duck, Crayon, Zebra and Moonlight, and every day he became a stronger and happier "crocoduck."